MY COUSIN THE KING

by Edward Frascino

Prentice-Hall, Inc.
Englewood Cliffs, New Jersey

For Elvira

Printed in Spain   ·J

Prentice-Hall International (UK) Limited, London
Prentice-Hall of Australia, Pty. Ltd., Sydney
Prentice-Hall Canada, Inc., Toronto
Prentice-Hall Hispanoamericana, S.A., Mexico
Prentice-Hall of India Private Ltd., New Delhi
Prentice-Hall of Japan, Inc., Tokyo
Prentice-Hall of Southeast Asia Pte. Ltd., Singapore
Whitehall Books Limited, Wellington, New Zealand
Editora Prentice-Hall do Brasil LTDA., Rio de Janeiro

10 9 8 7 6 5 4 3 2 1

Library of Congress Cataloging in Publication Data

Frascino, Edward.
   My cousin the king.

   Summary: A cat lords it over the other farmyard
animals through his boasts about being related to
the lion, until a visit to his royal cousin backfires.
   1. Children's stories, American. [1. Cats—Fiction.
2. Lions—Fiction. 3. Domestic animals—Fiction]
I. Title.
PZ7.F8596My 1985   [E]   85-3647
ISBN 0-13-608423-0

"Mice!" shrieked the farmer's wife. "Mice in my pantry. Mice in my parlor. Mice in my sewing basket. I need a cat!"

One day, soon afterward, the farmer was returning from town when he came upon a damp, droopy creature who was indeed a cat.

"What luck," he said to his mule, and he took the cat home to his wife.

After a saucer of warm milk and some leftover hash, the cat went to work. By week's end the mice had packed up and moved out of the farmhouse.

The farmer's wife rewarded the cat with a down-filled cushion.
"Home sweet home," he purred.

That evening after supper, the farmer's wife took down a volume
of the secondhand encyclopedia she'd bought at the church
bazaar.

"Just imagine! Everything you would ever want to know is in
these twenty volumes," she told her husband.

As the farmer sat smoking his pipe and the cat dozed on his cushion, the farmer's wife opened Volume *K* to her place marked with a chicken feather.

"King," she read aloud, "the supreme royal personage. No one is higher."

"One has to be born to that life," sighed the farmer.

"Lion," she read aloud some nights later from Volume *L*, "the most famous member of the cat family, called the King of Beasts."

The cat's ears perked up. "A member of my family is King of Beasts," he thought. "Therefore, I must be a royal personage, too."

That night he dreamed grand dreams.

The next morning, with his tail held high, the cat swaggered out
to the barnyard and climbed a fence post. The farm animals—a
pig, a cow, a sheep, some chickens, and a mule—all looked at him.

"Ahem!" the cat cleared his throat. "The lion is King of Beasts. And, as everyone knows, the lion is a large cat. That makes him my cousin."

"So what?" snorted the pig.

"I am a royal personage," declared the cat.

"Nonsense," interrupted the sheep.

The chickens clucked and chuckled and pecked at the ground.

"That's no way to treat royalty!" shouted the cat. "You bumpkins should learn some respect."

"Gosh," said the mule. "I'm happy to make your acquaintance, royal personage."

"At least one intelligent animal lives in this barnyard," said the cat.

The next time the farmer rode his mule to the store, he saw a poster. The Ding-a-Ling Brothers Traveling Circus had come to town.

"They've got a real-live lion," the storekeeper told the farmer.

"I've never seen you in such a hurry to get home," the farmer said as the mule trotted all the way back to the farm.

The mule told the cat what he had seen and heard. After supper, while the farmer and his wife sat in the parlor, the cat crept out to the barn and whispered something in the mule's ear. Without waking the other animals, the mule pushed open the barnyard gate. Then, with the cat on his back, he trotted off down the road.

The circus grounds were dark and quiet when the cat and mule arrived. Everyone was asleep except the lion, who was pacing to and fro in a fancy red-and-gold cage.

"Your Royal Highness," the cat said, trembling with excitement, "I, your royal cousin, salute you."

"Royal Highness?" wondered the lion. "Is he talking to me?"

"Your loyal subjects the pig, the cow, the sheep, and the chickens," continued the cat, "also wish to honor you."

"Livestock," thought the lion. "Yum-yum."

"Where are they?" he asked.

"On our farm in the valley," replied the cat, "and if we leave now we'll be there for breakfast."

The lion's mouth watered.

"Let's go, cousin," said the King of Beasts. "Just unlatch the door."

"Help me!" the cat commanded the mule, and together they lifted the heavy latch. The cage door swung open.

With a terrifying roar, the lion leaped to his freedom.

"Wait for me, your Majesty!" cried the cat as the lion disappeared into the darkness.

The frightened mule galloped for home, leaving the cat to walk all the way back alone.

At dawn the mule reached the farm and told the other animals what had happened. It was well past lunchtime when the cat arrived, tired and dusty. The pig snorted and glowered at him.

"Your cousin, his Royal Highness, is terrorizing the countryside," spoke out the cow.

"Well," said the cat, "nobody's perfect."

"If that's how royalty behaves, I'm glad to be a bumpkin," said the sheep.

The cat looked at the mule, who turned up his nose.

The following day a goose, honking and fluttering, ran into the barnyard. One of the chickens recognized her. "That's the goose from the farm next door."

"The lion attacked our farm last night," sputtered the goose. "He ate all the chickens, carried off the goat, and I just barely escaped his jaws." Then she collapsed in a faint.

"Help! Murder! Police!" babbled the chicken, running in circles. "Where can I hide? Where can I hide?"

That night, too frightened to sleep in their coop, the chickens joined the others in the barn. The goose asked if she could sleep there, too. They all agreed and made a comfortable straw bed for her in the hayloft.

"Leave a lamp lit," the farmer reminded his wife before going to bed. "We wouldn't want to trip over that lion if he shows up in the middle of the night."

Alone in the parlor, the cat shivered. He imagined every sound was the lion sneaking up.

He peeked out of the window and nearly screeched in terror. A huge, black-winged demon was flying around the barn. But before he could run and hide, the cat caught sight of a tiny moth fluttering around the lamp. It had cast a shadow a hundred times larger than itself on the side of the barn.

"Silly me," the cat smiled to himself.

All at once he heard a low rumble down by the chicken coop. His cat's eyes pierced the darkness, and he saw not a shadow but the lion himself.

"My cousin the king," he shuddered.

The lion sniffed the air. "Yum-yum." He licked his chops and turned toward the barn.

"I can't let him eat them," thought the cat in panic as the lion moved silently through the barnyard. "I must do something."

Sensing danger, the animals inside the barn trembled with fear. The goose had goose bumps.

The lion had almost reached the barn when suddenly he
stopped in his tracks and every hair of his mane stood on end.
Before him towered the biggest, meanest-looking monster he had
ever seen.

"Yipe!" he cried. Then he turned and ran.

The cat, feeling as big as his shadow, leaped out of the window after him.

"Scaredy-cat!" he shouted as the lion bounded over a hill.

From the hayloft window the goose saw everything.

"We're saved! That brave cat chased the lion away," she honked and fainted with relief.

The lion didn't stop running until he was back in his red-and-gold cage. He huddled in a corner, hoping someone would lock the door.

"Warm-blooded animals," the farmer's wife read from Volume *W.* "All birds and mammals, including human beings. Hair, fur, or feathers help to keep a warm-blooded animal warm."

"Can you ever forgive me?" pleaded the cat.
The farm animals talked it over.
"We forgive you," said the pig.

"But," added the mule, "no more visits from your relatives."

"You are all my relatives," smiled the cat. "We all belong to the warm-blooded animal family, even the farmer and his wife."

"Well, I declare," beamed the cow. "We're *all* cousins."

"Hi, cousin," everyone said at once, and the barnyard glowed with good cheer.

DATE DUE

NOV 20 '86	SEP 12 '89	MAR 2 '92	AUG 22 '94
DEC 8 '86	SEP 12 '89	MAR 23 '92	SEP 20 '94
MAR 9	SEP 12 '89	APR 10 '92	OCT 27 '94
MAR 9 '87	SEP 26 '89	APR 27 '92	NOV 11 '94
MAY 1 '87	OCT 16 '89	JUL 1 '92	MAR 21 '95
JUL 16 '87	NOV 6 '89	JUL 22 '92	MAY 30 '95
AUG 10 '87	NOV 29 '88	15 '92	JUL 2 '95
AUG 24 '87	21	DEC 1 '92	JUL 5 1995
JE 6 '88	28 '90	MAR 3 '93	OCT 13 '95
JUN 20 '89	JUL 23 '90	JUL 2 '93	16 1995
JY 6 '88	AUG 20 '90	AUG 30 '9	JAN 23
JUL 19	APR 2 '91	FEB 5 '94	FEB 3 '96
8 '89	JN 17 '91	MAY 8 '94	
AG 24 '88	JUL 10 '91	JUN 9 '94	
JUN 28 '89	AUG 3 '91	JUN 21 '94	
AUG 7 '89	AUG 12 '91	JUL 7 '94	
AUG 23 '89	JAN 25 '92	JUL 21 '94	

HIGHSMITH 45-102   PRINTED IN U.S.A.